Marshal Matt
and the
Slippery Snacks
Mystery

Nancy I. Sanders
Illustrated by Larry Nolte

CPH.
SAINT LOUIS

With love for my brother, Richard

Marshal Matt: Mysteries with a Value

Marshal Matt and the Slippery Snacks Mystery
Marshal Matt and the Topsy-Turvy Trail Mystery

Scripture quotations, unless otherwise indicated, taken from the HOLY BIBLE, NEW INTERNATIONAL VERSION®. NIV®. Copyright © 1973, 1978, 1984 by International Bible Society. Used by permission of Zondervan Publishing House. All rights reserved.

Copyright © 1996 Nancy I. Sanders
Published by Concordia Publishing House
3558 S. Jefferson Avenue, St. Louis, MO 63118-3968
Manufactured in the United States of America

Library of Congress Cataloging-in-Publication Data

Sanders, Nancy I.
    Marshall Matt and the slippery snacks mystery / Nancy Sanders : illustrated by Larry Nolte.
        p.   cm.   ——(Marshal Matt, mysteries with a value)
    Summary: Marshal Matt tries to find out who is stealing the snacks at vacation Bible school.
    ISBN 0-570-04769-X
    [1. Mystery and detective stories.   2. Honesty—Fiction. 3. Christian life—Fiction.] I. Nolte, Larry, ill. II. Title. III. Series: Sanders, Nancy I. Marshal Matt, mysteries with a value.
PZ7.S19784Mar   1996

[E]—dc20   96-10620

1 2 3 4 5 6 7 8 9 10   05 04 03 02 01 00 99 98 97 96

"HE WHO HAS BEEN STEALING MUST STEAL NO LONGER."
EPHESIANS 4:28

My friends call me Marshal
Matt. I solve mysteries. Today,
I was not solving a mystery. It was
Monday, the first day of vacation
Bible school. I was at church.

3

It was Bible memory verse time. "Ephesians 4:28," I started. "He who has been stealing ..."

Gr-r-r. Was that a bear? No. It was my tummy. I felt hungry enough to eat a bear. Snack time came next.

I tried to say my verse again. "He who has been stealing must steal no longer." I did it!

Just then Janie walked into our room. Her gray parrot, Blinky, sat on her shoulder.

"No snacks for your class today," Janie said.

Gr-r-r.

"Was that a bear?" Janie asked.

"No," I said. I rubbed my tummy. "Did you say there are no snacks?"

"Right," Janie said. "I got all the snacks ready. One tray of snacks for each room. I took each tray to the right room. When I went back to the kitchen, your tray was gone. Somebody stole your snacks!"

Blinky blinked. "Thief! Thief!" he squawked. He looked right at me.

I knew I was not the thief.

"Will you help me, Marshal Matt?" Janie asked.

Blinky blinked again. "Help! Help!" he said.

I reached in my shirt pocket. I pulled out my badge. I pinned my badge to my shirt. "I, Marshal Matt, will help solve this mystery."

I walked with Janie and Blinky.
We walked through an empty
room. Then we went into the
kitchen. Janie pointed to an empty
table.

"Your snack was on this table," Janie said. "The tray had juice, popcorn, and gummy worms. Now it's gone."

I pointed to another table. "What are these?" I asked.

"This is my rubber stamp," Janie said. "This is my stamp pad and paper. I made a card to put on each tray." Janie always tries to make things look nice.

"We are learning how God took care of Noah," Janie said. "I brought my rainbow stamp. I made a card with a rainbow for each tray."

Gr-r-r. I knew what that was.
"No more snacks?" I asked.

"No more snacks," Janie said.

I looked around. "I see bread," I said. "And raisins."

"What kind of snack is that?" Janie asked.

"A snack for a hungry person. Please fix a new tray for our room. I will look for the thief."

Blinky blinked at me. "Thief! Thief!" he squawked.

THIEF!
THIEF!

I crawled on the floor. I looked under the tables. I only saw a gummy worm.

I, Marshal Matt, stood up. "Ouch!" I bumped my head.

I looked in the refrigerator. I saw lots of carrots! I had put them there this morning. That reminded me. It was snack time for Mister E!

I grabbed some carrots. I headed outside. I, Marshal Matt, wanted to find Mister E.

Mister E is my horse. He stood in the parking lot under a tree. A green parrot sat on his shoulder. It nibbled on his ear. Two bunnies sat beside him. Dogs barked. Cats meowed. Everyone could bring their pet to vacation Bible school. The parking lot was Noah's ark.

Mister E neighed. I put the parrot back in its cage. "Hi, Mister E," I said. "Guess how many carrots I have."

Mister E stamped his foot one time.

"Nope," I said. "Guess again."

Mister E stamped his foot three times.

"Nope," I said. "Two!"

I fed the carrots to Mister E. I told him about the missing snacks. "Do you think I can find the thief today?" I asked.

Mister E wiggled his left ear. That's how he says no.

"I think you are right," I said. "I, Marshal Matt, will come back tomorrow."

On Tuesday, Janie came to get me. We were learning how God put a rainbow in the sky to promise He'd never destroy the earth again with a flood. "Time to fix the snacks," Janie said.

We walked through a room full of little kids. The kids were loud. Too loud! Three little boys played football. Two little girls played tag. Why weren't they learning about Noah?

Janie stopped in the middle of the room. "Hi, Fred," she said. Fred is Janie's baby brother. He always carries a blue toy hammer.

"Hi, hi!" Fred said. He pounded his hammer on my cowboy boot.

"Hi," I said. I rubbed my foot.

Blinky blinked. "Hi, Fly!" he squawked.

Fred giggled. We waved good-bye. We walked to the kitchen.

I, Marshal Matt, got right to work. "Show me everything you did on Monday," I said.

Janie put six trays on the table. "I use six trays. One tray for each room." She put milk and cookies on each tray.

Janie walked to the other table. She picked up her rainbow stamp. "I made a rainbow card for each tray," she said.

Janie picked up one tray. "Then I took the snacks to the rooms."

"I, Marshal Matt, will follow you," I said. "I will look for clues."

We took a tray to one room. We walked back to the kitchen. We took a tray to another room. We took all the trays to all the rooms except one. We walked back to get the last tray. It was gone!

"Thief! Thief!" Blinky squawked.

Janie and I ran back to all the rooms. We peeked inside. No extra trays. We looked in Fred's room. Empty! Was this a clue?

We went back to the kitchen.

"I will fix more snacks," Janie said.

"Thanks," I said. I grabbed some carrots. I needed to find Mister E.

Mister E was standing under the tree again. A cat was taking a bath on his back. A turtle was parked under him.

Mister E neighed. He was happy to see me. I moved the cat. I put the turtle back in his box.

I fed the carrots to Mister E. I told him about Fred's empty room.

"Is this a clue?" I asked. Mister E wiggled his right ear. That is how he says yes.

"Can I find the thief today?" I asked.

Mister E wiggled his left ear. No.

"I think you are right," I said. "I, Marshal Matt, will come back tomorrow."

On Wednesday, I was ready for snack time. I helped Janie put the snacks on the trays. Janie started to make rainbow cards again. She picked up her rainbow stamp.

"Stop!" I said. I pulled something out of my pocket.

"I, Marshal Matt, have a plan.
Last night, I made my own stamps.
Today we will put a different
picture on each card. We will put a
different card on each tray. When
the tray is gone, we can look in all
the rooms. We can find out which
tray is missing. Then we can look
for it."

Janie and I put a different card on each tray. We took the trays to each room. We walked back to the kitchen to get the last tray. Someone was in the kitchen! It was Pam!

"Thief! Thief!" Blinky squawked.

"Pam," I said, "what are you doing here?"

"I ran in here," Pam said. Pam always runs. She likes to run.

"I ran in here to tell you that we need two extra snacks," Pam said. "You weren't here. I ran to get two cups of juice. I put the juice on the tray. There was only one tray."

Pam pointed to the table. Juice
was on the table. And a wet card. "I
spilled the juice. The card got wet. I
put the card on the table to dry."

Pam held up a bunch of paper towels. "I ran to the bathroom. I got some paper towels. I ran back. The tray was gone!"

I looked at the wet card. The card was still here! My plan didn't work.

On Thursday I had another plan. Janie and I spooned chocolate pudding into little cups. We put the cups on the trays. We made one extra tray.

In each cup of pudding on one tray, we put gummy bugs. In each cup of pudding on another tray, we put gummy dinosaurs. In all the pudding on each different tray, we put a different kind of candy. On the last tray, we put gummy worms in all the pudding.

Blinky blinked. He hopped off Janie's arm. He walked across the table. He reached over to the last tray. He ate a gummy worm.

"Blinky!" Janie said. She put him back on her shoulder.

We took six different trays to six different rooms. We came back to the kitchen. The extra tray was gone!

"Come on," I said.

Janie and I peeked in all the rooms. Kids in the first room were eating gummy dinosaurs. Kids in the last room were eating gummy bugs. Nobody was eating gummy worms! The tray with the gummy worms was missing!

Janie and I looked in Fred's room. It was empty. We looked in all the other rooms in the church. They were all empty. There were no gummy worms anywhere!

Janie and I walked back to the kitchen. "What are we going to do, Marshal Matt?" Janie asked.

I needed to think. "Come with me," I said. I grabbed three carrots. We headed out to Noah's ark. I wanted to see Mister E.

Janie and I fed carrots to Mister E. "Are all those empty rooms a clue?" I asked. Mister E wiggled his right ear. Yes.

Just then we heard a loud noise. Rich walked over to us. He was wearing a bright yellow shirt that said *Day Care*.

Rich was carrying Fred. Fred was crying. Fred was making the loud noise.

Janie took Fred in her arms. "What happened?"

"Fred was running," Rich said. "He fell down. He hurt his big toe."

Fred stopped crying. He held up his big toe.

Blinky blinked. "Goo goo got a boo boo," he squawked. Fred giggled.

Rich left. Janie sat down on the ground. Fred sat down on her lap. Blinky sat down on her shoulder.

"Look!" I said. I pointed to Fred.

In one fist, Fred held his blue toy hammer. In the other fist, Fred held a gummy worm. He had chocolate pudding on his face!

I looked at Mister E. "More clues?" I asked. Mister E wiggled his right ear. Yes.

I thought about the clues. Empty kitchen. Empty rooms. Day care. Fred. Gummy worms.

"I, Marshal Matt, have solved the mystery!" I said.

"But who stole the snacks?" Janie asked. "And who was the thief?"

"There was no thief," I said. "Come with me."

We walked around to the back of the church. Lots of little kids ran around on the grass.

Rich walked up to us. "Is your toe better, Fred?" he asked.

Blinky blinked. "Fredder is better," he squawked. Fred giggled.

I looked at Janie. "Rich is too old to come to vacation Bible school. Fred is too little. All these boys and girls are too little to come to vacation Bible school."

"That's right," Janie said. "Fred goes to day care."

I pointed to Rich's shirt. "Rich helps out in the day care."

Rich nodded his head. "Working with these little guys is great."

"Fred ate gummy worms in his chocolate pudding today," I said. "Every day, the day care kids eat snacks. Every day, the day care kids come on the grass to eat their snacks. That is why Fred's room is empty."

"Most of the time I make our snacks," Rich said. "But this week, someone nice made them for me. Every day, there was a tray of food on the table in the kitchen."

"See?" I said. "There was no thief. It was all a mistake."

Janie smiled. "On Friday, we are having a pizza party. I will make a tray of pizza for day care too."

I, Marshal Matt, grinned. I like pizza the best. Especially right after I solve a mystery.

Hey, kids! Join me in my Marshal Matt Cowpoke Club! Remember: You're special! God loves you so much, He sent His Son, Jesus, to die for you. He will help you be an honest cowpoke. You can solve mysteries with me! Just write your name on the blank.

With Jesus' help,

I, _____,

will be an honest member of the Marshal Matt Cowpoke Club!

As a member of my club, you can make your very own Marshal Matt stamps! Turn the page to find out how.

Ask an adult to help you cut a foam tray (like the ones that meat and fruit come on) into two-inch squares. Draw a simple picture on each square. Slowly press your pencil deeper into the foam on all the lines you draw. You just made a stamp!

Rub your picture back and forth across a stamp pad. Then press it on a piece of paper. Try it again—and again. Have fun making more pictures. You never know. You might need your stamps to solve a mystery—like me!

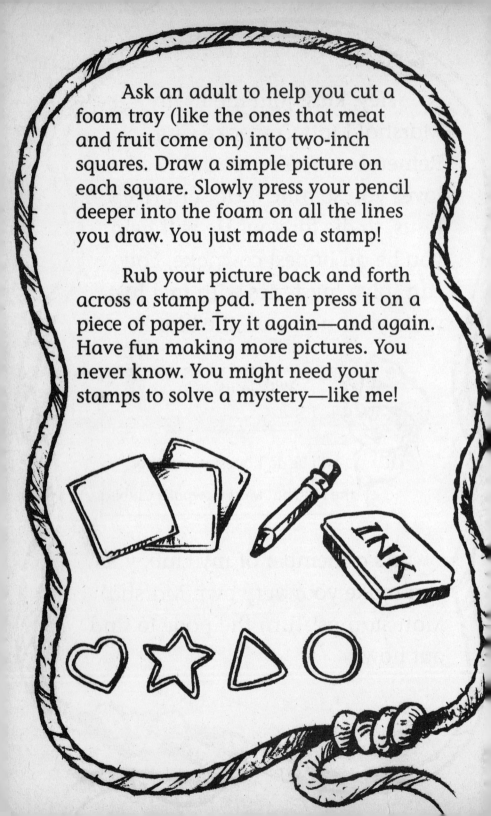